Not A Nugget

Written by Stephanie Dreyer

Illustrations by Jack Veda

NOT A NUGGET By Stephanie Dreyer
ISBN 978-0-9861060-1-9

Book design and illustrations by Jack Veda

FIRST EDITION

For Dave, who rules my roost,
and our amazing chicks, Gaby, Alex and Jake.

Foreword

When I first met Stephanie, her passion for animals and her dedication to educating children about plant-based eating struck me as special.

Most children have a natural connection with animals, but few make the connection between their love for animals and the habit of eating them. Engaging children early in the discussion about the origins of our food, and the impact on ourselves, animals and environment is critical. Presenting this information in an engaging and fun way is challenging, but Stephanie has done it in *Not A Nugget*. With each page turn, she invites children and families to connect with animals in healthy and positive ways, and that means not eating them. She explains that animals, just like us, want to avoid pain and suffering, and she encourages children to think differently about what they choose to eat.

But, she doesn't stop there. Stephanie has provided additional resources, recipes, and articles (all accessible on her fabulous website, VeegMama.com) to help families on their plant-based journeys. *Not A Nugget* is a fun, inspired look at the food on our plates and the beautiful animals who want to be our friends, not our food. Children will enjoy the illustrations and interesting animal facts that connect them. This entertaining read is a unique, educational tool to teach kids about plant-based eating at home and in schools.

I am grateful for this special book.

- Gene Baur, Founder Farm Sanctuary

Not a nugget.

Did you know that chickens like to play games just like us?

If you give a small group of chickens a ball or an apple,
they will pass it around and play their own version of "football" together.

Not a hamburger.

Did you know that cows have best friends too?

They take walks together and travel in herds like families.
They form deep friendships and strong family bonds.

Not a hot dog.

Did you know that pigs are super smart?

They are smarter than dogs and 3 year-old kids.
They can learn to play video games with a joystick
and can also learn their names!

Not an omelet.

Did you know that mama chickens talk to their chicks before they hatch just like your mom did when you were in her belly?

Mama chicken recognizes different peeps to know if her chicks are cold or comfortable. By the time they hatch, chicks know mama's voice just like human babies do.

Not a sandwich.

Did you know that fish communicate and make friends like we do?

Instead of words, they use gurgles, squeaks, squeals, and other sounds.

Not a steak.

Did you know that cows are problem solvers?

They get excited when they figure out a solution and
have been known to learn how to unlock a gate that leads to food,
and push the lever on a drinking fountain.

Not a fish stick.

Did you know that fish have memories like us?

Fish recognize their mates and can retain information,
such as how to escape a net, for their entire lives
once they have been exposed to the experience.

Not a marshmallow.

Did you know that horses are loyal friends and form long-term bonds just like us?

They recognize humans after having been separated from them for over 8 months.

Not soup.

Did you know that clams live longer than us?

If left alone in their original habitats,
clams can live up to several hundred years!

Not a stew.

Did you know that rabbits have a sense of smell
that is far better than ours?

They use their nose to detect signs of trouble or danger.

Not sushi.

Did you know that fish have amazing senses?

Just like we feel, so do fish,
but fish feel nearby objects without even touching them!

Not Thanksgiving dinner.

Did you know that turkeys sing?

If you turn on a radio, they will gather around
and give you a "concert," gobbling along to the music!

Animals are our friends,

not food.

Other Fun Facts About Our Friends:

Turkeys have really good eyesight
and can see colors that we cannot.

Chickens are so smart that they can learn to open doors
and turn off the heat when they want to cool down.

Pigs can be taught to fetch and
change the temperature on a thermostat.

Cows have strong memories
and can remember where things are located.

Pigs can recognize each other's snorts
and whistles from far away.

Horses have excellent memories.
They can remember how to solve a
difficult problem for over 10 years.

Rabbits can hear up to a mile away.

What else can we eat?

Instead of a hot dog, eat a veggie wrap.

Instead of a hamburger, eat a black bean burger.

Instead of bacon, eat tempeh bacon.

Instead of scrambled eggs, eat a tofu scramble.

Instead of a sushi roll, eat a cucumber and avocado roll.

Author's Note:

Gelatin is an animal product made from boiling animal skin, hooves, tendons, ligaments, and cartilage. It is obtained from cows, pigs, fish, and horses, and is used as a thickener in marshmallows, gelatin desserts, puddings, and candy.

Please visit *http://veegmama.com* for recipes, as well as classroom and home resources to explore plant-based eating with children.

Made in the USA
Middletown, DE
15 December 2019